LOVE MAGIC

by Marla Hughes

illustrated by David Molinero

WORDS MATTER

P U B L I S H I N G

OUR WORDS CHANGE THE WORLD

Words Matter Publishing
P.O. Box 531
Salem, Il 62881
www.wordsmatterpublishing.com

ISBN 13: 978-1-953912-11-4

Library of Congress Catalog Card Number: 2021938617

Dedication

I dedicate this book to my children
Dean, Matt, and Carly, also known as
Yoyo, Tiger, and Buttercup

"The most important things in life are not seen with the eyes but felt with the heart."

Note from the Author

I believe that the world would be forever changed if children were taught that their loved ones who have passed (pets included) are not lost. Instead, they are here for us to connect with through feelings, memories, rituals, symbolic gestures, signs and love.

This book was written for adults as well as children. I envision a little one listening to the words of this story and being filled with wonder as their caregiver helps them to continue a beautiful relationship with those who have entered a new dimension, a different frequency. I believe that when a child is taught that these love connections are possible, and that there is something in the universe that is bigger and more wondrous than what we see on earth, an inner strength develops. I like to call it the divine. When a child is sad or lonely, how amazing it would be for them to feel that they have a guardian angel looking over them, offering a hand to hold, an arm to lean on, someone who is there for them without judgement. And to know that they can still laugh, love, ask questions or just be quiet with their loved one who is now in spirit.

I wrote this book because I want children to live in love instead of fear when someone they love passes. I want them to know that those special connections though not visible to the eye, are known to be true in the heart. My hope is that this book will bring comfort to all of us, no matter where we are.

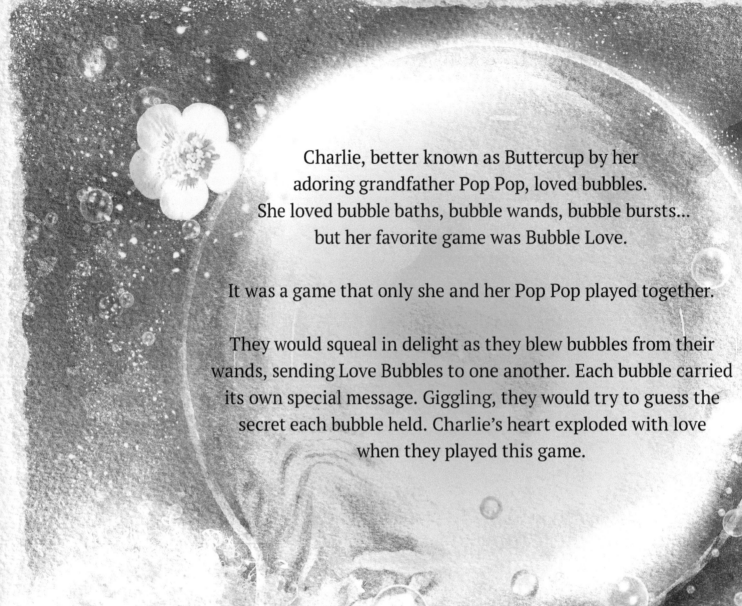

Charlie, better known as Buttercup by her
adoring grandfather Pop Pop, loved bubbles.
She loved bubble baths, bubble wands, bubble bursts...
but her favorite game was Bubble Love.

It was a game that only she and her Pop Pop played together.

They would squeal in delight as they blew bubbles from their
wands, sending Love Bubbles to one another. Each bubble carried
its own special message. Giggling, they would try to guess the
secret each bubble held. Charlie's heart exploded with love
when they played this game.

One Saturday afternoon a few months later,
Charlie and Cosmo, her adorable puppy, were in
the garden of her grandmother's cottage. This was
her special day to be with Gramma, and they were
planting lavender.

Charlie was struggling to use a big hoe, and her garden
boots were caked with dirt. She loved being with Gramma,
who was gentle and kind. Stopping to wipe the sweat from
her eyes, Charlie gazed up at the sun peeking through
the clouds.

"Thinking or dreaming, Charlie?" asked Gramma.

"Both, Gramma," Charlie answered wistfully.

"I feel all dreamy in my heart when I think of Pop Pop's
sky-blue eyes and remember his whistling."

Her beloved Pop Pop had gone to heaven not long ago.

Charlie couldn't stop thinking about her grandfather.

She loved him dearly and was really missing him.
He had twinkly blue eyes and was always whistling.

He also made the yummiest waffles
        in the entire universe
            and always piled

    whipped cream
            on top with
                    strawberries

        from the garden.

Taking a break from her hoeing, Charlie lay down on the ground and gazed up at the clouds. She noticed some sprinkles of rain were dropping on her forehead. Charlie loved the rain. Pop Pop had loved the rain too. He said it cleaned Mother Earth so all of her beautiful creations could blossom.

Once, she and Pop Pop had gone out in the pouring rain together, just to see how it felt.

They had splashed about and danced.

It was magical!

Feeling the magic of the moment, Gramma went and sat down with Charlie.

"Remember when Pop Pop called you his precious Buttercup and told you that once he is in heaven, all you need to do is think of him, and he'll be there with you?"

"Oh yes, Gramma," Charlie replied.

"He said, 'I am only one Buttercup thought away.'"

"What else did Pop Pop say to you?"

"He said we feel the most important things in the world in our hearts. We don't need to see them with our eyes. He told me that's what it means to believe."

"And do you believe?" Charlie's big eyes looked troubled.

"I think so, Gramma,"
she said slowly,

"But how does it work?"

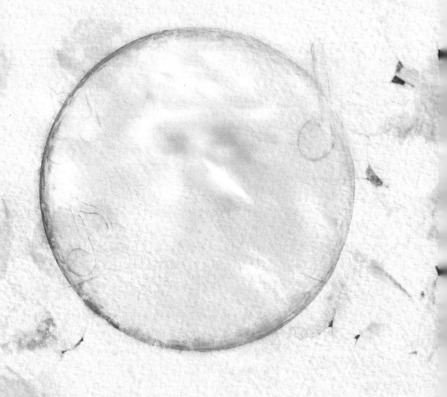

Gramma sat up and looked at Charlie with a smile. "Let's do it together now. Close your eyes and think of Pop Pop's twinkling blue eyes and the smell of his waffles and his beautiful whistling."

"Oh yes, Gramma," Charlie said excitedly, sitting up too. "I can feel his Love Bubbles in my heart and ... wait ... there are Buttercups all around him. I can see his eyes and hear his whistle in my heart and.. ooooohhhh...those waffles smell so good!"

"Well, this is how you connect with those you love, wherever they may be. I call it 'Love Magic'."

Charlie understood perfectly what her grandmother was saying. "Even though heaven is invisible, Gramma, when I close my eyes I can see it!"

"Yes, Charlie. Not only can you see it, you can feel it."

They sat together in silence then, looking at the softly falling rain. After a while, Charlie asked, "Gramma, what do you think it is like in heaven?"

"Pop Pop says to me, through his feelings and mine, that heaven is full of light, beauty, color, music and love -more than we can possibly imagine. I can feel his pure happiness and joy."

Gramma's answer made Charlie smile. It was wonderful to know Pop Pop was somewhere so full of light and love. But one thing still puzzled her. "How do you know this, Gramma?"

"Through the Love Bubbles, Charlie. Each time you think of anyone you love in heaven, you send a Love Bubble to their heart and they send one back.

Then the magic happens."

Charlie noticed the rain was beginning to come down a little harder. "Do you have an umbrella, Gramma?" she asked.

"Sure do," Gramma said with a wink.
"Don't I always come prepared?"

Gramma got up and rummaged around in
the bag she'd brought out with her.
Then she held up the stripy umbrella Charlie
had given her for Christmas last year.

Linking arms and sheltering underneath it,
the two of them walked back to the cottage.

It was warm and cozy in the farmhouse kitchen.
Charlie and Gramma sat at the table having milk
and chocolate chip cookies as they watched the rain
pouring down outside onto Mother Earth.

Charlie loved the cookies. She adored how they tasted
sugary and chocolatey at the same time, especially
when she dipped them in her milk.
"One last thing to tell you, Charlie," said Gramma,
brushing a flaky crumb from her lip.

"When people are in heaven, they send
their loved ones signs that they are
looking over them and are
always with them."

23

Charlie was thrilled by this wonderful news and wanted to know more. "What do you mean by signs?" she asked.

"Well, remember how much Pop Pop LOVED his hummingbirds?"

"Yes!" Charlie replied excitedly. "He used to sit in his rocking chair and whistle to them in the red feeder he built."

"Well now," Gramma went on, "I know whenever I see a hummingbird that it is Pop Pop sending me love and letting me know he is right here."

Charlie clapped her hands with delight.

"So you're saying Pop Pop sends the hummingbird as a messenger to say how much he loves us and is always there for us?"

"Exactly! Well done, Charlie."

Charlie had not seen a hummingbird since she last sat in this very kitchen with Pop Pop. She remembered munching popcorn and drinking lemonade as she watched his two hummingbirds sipping sugar water from their red drinking bottle.

Gramma and Charlie sat down on the couch in the lounge and
snuggled up under a fluffy comforter. This was their special cozy spot.

"Do you want to try the Love Magic again?" asked Gramma.

Charlie jumped up and down, clapping her hands.
"Yes please, Gramma!"

"Okay, then. Close your eyes and think of Pop Pop."

Charlie pictured him with his fancy red jacket on,
dancing to his favorite music.
She leaped up and ran to his old record player.
"Wait, wait! Can we play one of Pop Pop's favorite tunes?
I know he would really love to hear the music right now!"

As the notes floated through the air, Charlie whispered,

"Gramma, Gramma! I feel him.
I feel him patting me on the head
like he always did.
I feel the LOVE he is sending me..."

The next morning, Charlie woke up early. She was excited because Gramma had said she could take Cosmo, her puppy, out for a walk all by herself.

"You're old enough now," Gramma had told her at bedtime. "It's a big responsibility, but I know you're up to it."

Mother Earth had come alive overnight. Charlie felt the trees singing, the birds were singing back, the flowers were blossoming and there was an explosion of color everywhere. She wondered if this is what heaven is like ... until Cosmo gave a sudden bark and chased after a rabbit. The leash jerked out of Charlie's hand, and she watched in dismay as the dog ran off.

"Cosmo! Cosmo, please come back, girl!"
she shouted, scrambling after her.

Cosmo had completely disappeared and Charlie felt panic rising in her throat at the thought of telling Gramma. She raced round a corner and there was Cosmo, jumping up at a fence with a hole in the bottom through which the bunny had escaped. Charlie rushed over and grabbed a hold of her leash.

Then she saw something that made her drop to her knees. She felt a happy tear slip down her cheek.

A hummingbird had flown down and was perched on one of the fence posts. It was the most beautiful hummingbird Charlie had EVER seen! Holding Cosmo tightly in her arms, she gazed up at the bird feeling her heart was about to explode. "This is a loving message from Pop Pop, Cosmo," she whispered.

"He's saying he's always been with me and will still be with me forever and ever." Charlie held Cosmo perfectly still so as not to scare the hummingbird away. They gazed in silence at the magical creature until it flew off, heading up into the sky in the direction of heaven.

Charlie suddenly realized what had happened.

"This was a sign from Pop Pop—just like Gramma had explained."

And at that moment, SHE BELIEVED. Her doubts were all gone.
She had understood what Gramma had told her and now it had
come true for her.
Charlie's head was reeling, and she gave Cosmo a long,
excited cuddle. The dog could feel her great joy and licked
her face repeatedly.

Then it was time to go home. Cosmo and Charlie
skipped back down the road together, feeling like
they were floating on air.

They were sure they could hear Pop Pop whistling the entire way.

Charlie knew it was him.

Meet the Author

Marla Hughes has worked with children her entire life in a number of different capacities. At the transplant unit of UCSF Hospital in San Francisco she taught children about exercise, nutrition and relaxation. She worked with Dr. Gerald Jampolsky at the Center for Attitudinal Healing, using art and music therapy to help young children who had life threatening diseases or who had a parent or loved one who was severely ill.

Her podcast, Interviews with Innocence (interviewswithinnocence.com), features experts in the fields of science and metaphysics who focus on children and spirituality. Marla is the founder of the Ethiopian Family Fund (ethiopianfamilyfund.org), a nonprofit dedicated to developing sustainable education and healthcare for Ethiopian children and their families. According to Marla, "My greatest teachers have been my children. I have never experienced a love that deep or profound."

Let's Connect:

 interviewswithinnocence

 @interviewswithinnocence

 @interviews_with

www.InterviewswithInnocence.com

Acknowledgements

I would like to express my deepest gratitude to the following people who assisted, inspired and supported me in the creation of "Love Magic":

To Teresa Bruno for her love, inspiration, intuition and her heart, to Laura Knight for being with me at the very beginning of this project and for her never-ending support, to Carly Hodes, my wonderful daughter who worked tirelessly to help me tell this story, to Kim Blue, website and editing consultant extraordinaire, for her enduring friendship and her enthusiasm for every new project I create, to Levi Anderson for his hard work and excitement for this project and all that I do, to my husband Dan, for always believing in me, to my son Matt for always lifting me up by telling me how proud he is of his mama and for loving my cooking, to my son Dean who has truly taught me that the most important things in life are not seen with the eyes but are felt with the heart, to Daisy and Cosmo, my two adorable labradoodles for their unconditional love and for bringing laughter into my life daily, and to Brian for more reasons than I can even begin to explain. To my illustrator, David Molinero, for his amazing creative talent and patience. To my Mom who is always there for me and taught me the importance of kindness. She is my angel.